OLIVIA™
Helps Mother Nature

adapted by Lauren Forte
based on the screenplay written by Patricia Resnick
illustrated by Jared Osterhold

Ready-to-Read

Simon Spotlight
New York   London   Toronto   Sydney   New Delhi

Based on the TV series OLIVIA™ as seen on Nickelodeon™

SIMON SPOTLIGHT
An imprint of Simon & Schuster Children's Publishing Division
1230 Avenue of the Americas, New York, New York 10020
OLIVIA™ Ian Falconer Ink Unlimited, Inc. and © 2014 Ian Falconer and Classic Media, LLC
For information about special discounts for bulk purchases, please contact Simon & Schuster Special Sales at
1-866-506-1949 or business@simonandschuster.com.
Manufactured in the United States of America 1213 LAK
First Edition 1 2 3 4 5 6 7 8 9 10
ISBN 978-1-4424-9664-4 (pbk)
ISBN 978-1-4424-9665-1 (hc)
ISBN 978-1-4424-9666-8 (eBook)

"What are you doing?"
asks Ian.
"I am recycling to help
Mother Nature," says Olivia.

"The bins are for things
we are finished using,"
Olivia says.
"Old glass, paper, and plastic
get made into other things."

"Cool," Ian answers. "Now, time for Operation Mother Nature!" says Olivia.

Olivia takes her dad's
newspaper.

Olivia turns out a light.
"Did the power go out?"
asks Mom.

"Hey!" yells Ian as Olivia turns off a faucet. "Save water!" Olivia cries.

Dad finds his paper.
"Olivia, recycling is great,
but please let me finish
reading first."

"We are going out for dinner," says Mom. "Please get into the car."

"Can we walk?" Olivia asks. "It is better for Mother Nature if we do not use gas."

"If we took the car we, would not have seen this beautiful starry sky," says Dad with a smile.

At bedtime, Ian wants
to keep his light on.
He does not like the dark.
"But that wastes electricity!"
cries Olivia.

Olivia wants to help.
She tries to make a
glowing helmet.
It does not work.

Olivia tells Ian that if
he keeps the light off,
he can knock on the wall for
her if he gets scared.
Ian knocked all night.

The next morning they are very tired.

"We need a new idea," Olivia says.

"You can say that again," answers Ian.

"How about a flashlight?" asks Ian.

"No. That uses up batteries," says Olivia.

"I need to think."

"Of course! Fireflies!"
Olivia cries.

"We will let them out
in the morning
and get new ones
tomorrow night," Olivia says.

I can sleep with the light off!" says Ian.

"I am proud of you for doing so much to save energy," says Dad.

"Thanks, Dad. Good night," says Olivia.

"And please turn off my light."